Skeletons Don't Play Tubas

There are more books about the Bailey School Kids!
Have you read these adventures?

Vampires Don't Wear Polka Dots
Santa Claus Doesn't Mop Floors
Leprechauns Don't Play Basketball
Werewolves Don't Go to Summer Camp
Ghosts Don't Eat Potato Chips
Frankenstein Doesn't Plant Petunias
Aliens Don't Wear Braces
Genies Don't Ride Bicycles
Pirates Don't Wear Pink Sunglasses
Witches Don't Do Backflips

Skeletons Don't Play Tubas

by **Debbie Dadey**
and
Marcia Thornton Jones

illustrated by John Steven Gurney

A
LITTLE APPLE
PAPERBACK

SCHOLASTIC INC.

New York   Toronto   London   Auckland   Sydney

To Marcia from Debbie
To Debbie from Marcia
— from one old bag of bones to another

ISBN 0-590-48113-4

12 11 10 9 8 7 6 5 4   5 6 7 8 9/9

Printed in the U.S.A.   40

First Scholastic printing, October 1994

Book design by Laurie Williams

Contents

1

Bailey City Cemetery

"Boo!" Eddie jumped out from behind a big tree and waved his baseball cap.

"Eddie!" Liza screamed, grabbing her friend Melody. "You scared me to death!"

"I told you it was a mean thing to do," Howie said, coming from behind the same tree.

"You guys are as jumpy as cats on Halloween," Eddie said, pulling his cap down over his curly red hair.

Melody shook her black braids. "You didn't scare me, but you have to admit this place *is* creepy."

It was early in the morning and the four friends were in the Bailey City Cemetery collecting leaves for a school project. Huge trees filled the cemetery and large red and yellow leaves littered the ground.

1

"But it is the best place to collect leaves," Howie said, holding up a handful of brightly colored leaves. "I bet I have ten different kinds already."

"Look at this one," Liza said, holding up an orange leaf. "It's really different."

"Talk about different, look over there." Eddie pointed. "That has to be the strangest-looking fellow I've ever seen."

The four kids looked at a very tall, very skinny man. He was holding a huge black box and walking toward them.

"I have never seen anyone so skinny," Melody said.

"Or so pale," Liza added. "He looks half dead."

"Maybe he is dead." Eddie snickered. "After all, we're in the cemetery."

Liza shivered. "His box is bigger than he is."

Eddie giggled again. "That's probably his coffin."

Just then the skinny man looked at the four kids and smiled, showing huge yellow teeth.

"Let's go!" Liza squealed and ran out of the cemetery. Her three friends followed her as fast as they could. The tall, skinny man was coming toward them.

2

Skeletons in the Closet

Eddie, Melody, Liza, and Howie raced all the way to Bailey Elementary School. They stopped under their favorite oak tree to rest.

"Why did you run?" Eddie asked Liza.

Melody agreed. "That man must think we're rude."

"I'd rather be really rude than really dead." Liza shuddered. "That guy gave me the creeps."

Howie nodded. "He is a stranger. We shouldn't talk to strangers."

"Especially ones that follow us!" Eddie said. He pointed to the stranger lugging his huge black box up the stairs of Bailey Elementary.

"Let's see what he's up to," Melody

suggested as the skinny man disappeared inside the school.

The four friends climbed the steps to Bailey Elementary. It was early in the morning, and no other students had arrived yet. They made their way silently down the hall until they could peek into the office. That's where they saw the tall skinny stranger talking to their principal, Mr. Davis. Principal Davis was a large, bald, egg-shaped man.

"If Principal Davis sat on that guy, he'd be chalk dust." Eddie laughed.

Melody smiled. "Mrs. Jeepers always needs more chalk. Maybe she could just use that fellow's bald head."

Eddie slapped Melody on the back. "If there were any more bald men around here we could start a baldy circus. We'd get rich selling tickets."

"It's not nice to make fun," Liza said as Principal Davis looked their way.

"Students, I'm glad you're here," he

said, pulling them toward the thin stranger. "I'd like you to meet the new band teacher, Mr. Belgrave. He is going to teach us how to play instruments."

Melody and Howie smiled at the new teacher, but Eddie looked at Principal Davis and said, "We've never had a band teacher before."

"Then it's about time!" Principal Davis slapped Mr. Belgrave on the shoulder. "Our new teacher is a real trouper. He is going to teach in the old science room, otherwise known as the storage closet."

"In the closet?" Liza asked.

Principal Davis nodded. "Since the school's so crowded, it was the only place to put the band class."

Mr. Belgrave smiled. His big yellow teeth stood out against his pale white skin. For the first time, the kids heard him speak. His voice came from deep inside his chest. "I look forward to seeing you in band class."

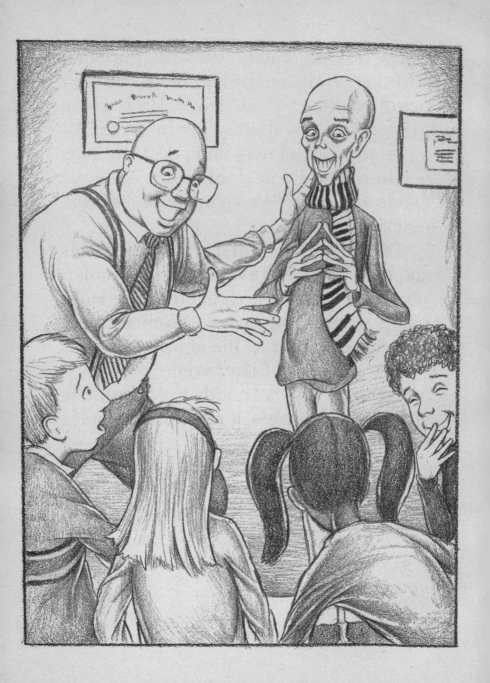

The four kids backed away and hurried down the hall toward their classroom. Eddie stopped before he went inside the room. "There's no way I'm going to learn music from that fellow. He looks like somebody sucked all the life out of him!"

"Maybe it was Mrs. Jeepers," Howie said, half-seriously. Many kids in their third-grade class thought that their teacher might be a vampire.

Melody shook her head. "Mr. Belgrave has probably been sick. He can't help it if he looks like death warmed over."

"I know he can't help it," Liza complained, "but he scares me. He looks just like a skeleton."

"Right," Eddie said seriously. "Just like a skeleton in a closet."

3

Moaning

"These are hard to make," Melody said. The whole third-grade class was making leaf print place mats to sell at the Fall Festival.

"It's stupid," Eddie said. "Adults are always thinking up hair-brained ideas to keep us busy."

"I wish we could make jack-o'-lanterns for Halloween instead of these things." Liza sighed.

"Shhh, Mrs. Jeepers might hear," Howie whispered, pointing to their teacher.

But Mrs. Jeepers did hear. She looked up from the papers she was grading and said in her Transylvanian accent, "I do not care to be associated with jack-o'-lanterns. They were originally used to ward off the dead. These place mats are much more cheerful." Mrs. Jeepers smiled her odd half smile and then went back to grading papers.

Howie nodded and held up a bright orange leaf. "We have to remember it's for a good cause, to make money for the school."

Eddie shrugged. "I just don't feel like making place mats."

Melody wiped paint off her fingers. "Nobody wants to make these, but we have to. So get busy!"

"I don't *have* to do anything!" Eddie smiled and tapped the pile of leaves on his desk. "Oooops!" he said as yellow leaves fluttered to the floor. "I'd better pick these up."

Eddie dropped to the floor and slowly began collecting his leaves. While he was crawling around, he tied the shoestrings of a girl named Carey to her chair and put Liza's book in Melody's desk.

Eddie was crumbling up a yellow leaf for Howie's notebook when the noise started. It started like a low hum. Then it grew louder and louder until the windows rattled.

"What is that?" Howie gulped. Liza's eyes got big and Melody's mouth dropped open.

"It sounds like a snoring elephant," Eddie said.

All the kids looked at Mrs. Jeepers in time to see her odd little half smile. "The new band teacher must be warming up his tuba," she said. "Which reminds me. It is time for us to have band class."

"Band class?" Eddie jumped up into his seat. "We have to go to band class?"

"Yes." Mrs. Jeepers smiled and rubbed the green brooch at her neck. "We are very fortunate that everyone may participate by playing an instrument. I am sure you will enjoy it. Now, line up."

"I'd rather eat wool coats," Eddie mumbled as he got up from his seat.

Mrs. Jeepers flashed her eyes at Eddie. "Did you say something?" she asked.

Eddie gulped and lied. "I said, I can't wait to play some notes."

The kids were quiet as their class walked down the hall to the new band room. Mrs. Jeepers watched as her class silently filed into the tiny room.

The room was crammed full of chairs and instruments. There were drums, violins, saxophones, flutes, trumpets, and a huge tuba that hung on the wall. Liza didn't notice the instruments, though. She was too busy staring at what was standing beside the tuba.

It was large. It was white. It was a skeleton!

4

Claude

"This is my good friend, Claude," Mr. Belgrave smiled, showing his big yellow teeth as he patted the skeleton on the head.

"Your friend?" Liza gulped and tried to scoot her chair away from Claude.

Mr. Belgrave nodded. "I couldn't find anyplace to put him, so I just left him here so he could enjoy the music."

"I don't think his ears work very well," Eddie teased.

Mr. Belgrave's teeth flashed another big smile. "Oh, you never know. Claude may be a real music lover. But enough about him, let's begin by passing out the instruments."

In just a few minutes, Mrs. Jeepers and Mr. Belgrave had helped almost everyone

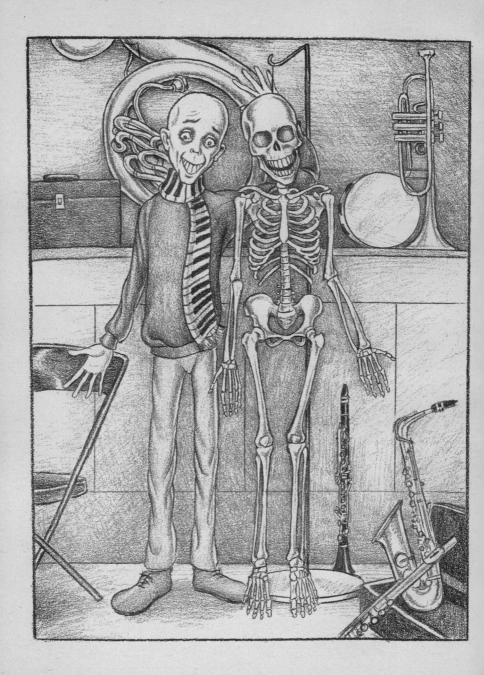

choose an instrument. Melody examined her flute as Liza tried out the valves on her saxophone. Howie tried to figure out how to hold his trombone, but Eddie had already figured out how to work the cymbals. *Cling! Cling!* Everyone's ears rang with the sound.

Cling! Cling! Eddie was having a great time clashing the cymbals together. *Cling! Cling!* Mr. Belgrave blinked twice and tapped his conductor's wand on a music stand, trying to get Eddie's attention. But Eddie couldn't hear him over the clanging cymbals. *Cling!*

When Mrs. Jeepers flashed her eyes in Eddie's direction, the rest of the class froze. Melody kicked his shin to get him to stop.

"What's the big idea?" Eddie asked. "I was just getting warmed up."

Mr. Belgrave smiled his big toothy grin and finished giving out the instruments. "No one wants the tuba?" he asked. "It's just as well. It's the only instrument I can't play."

"Really?" Mrs. Jeepers looked surprised. "I was certain I heard tuba music earlier."

Mr. Belgrave shook his bald head. "It wasn't me."

"Maybe it was Claude," Eddie piped up.

Mr. Belgrave smiled. "Maybe it was."

"Students," Mrs. Jeepers said, walking out the door. "I leave you in Mr. Belgrave's capable hands. I am sure you will give him your complete attention."

Mr. Belgrave smiled and picked up his conductor's wand. "Let's begin," he said in a low voice.

"But we don't know the first thing about these instruments," Melody said. "You can't seriously expect us to play."

Mr. Belgrave looked deep into her eyes. "I am dead serious," he told her and motioned for everyone to begin.

A squeaking, honking, banging sound

filled the air. By the end of the hour, Mr. Belgrave had given each student a few tips on playing their instrument, and the noise almost sounded like music.

"I felt like I was really playing in there." Howie smiled as they walked back to their classroom.

"I never knew music could be such fun," Melody agreed.

Eddie nodded. He'd had a great time banging the cymbals, but he noticed Liza hadn't said a word. "What's wrong?" he asked her. "Skeleton got your tongue?"

Howie gasped and Melody shrieked when they looked at their friend. Liza's skin was deathly pale.

5

Toe-tapping Tunes

Liza tugged Melody's arm, pulling her down a side hall. Eddie and Howie followed close behind. When they lost sight of the rest of the class, Liza gathered her three friends in a tight huddle.

"What's gotten into you?" Melody asked. "You act like you've seen a ghost."

"It wasn't exactly a ghost. But it sure was dead," Liza said, her eyes wide.

"What are you mumbling about?" Eddie snapped. "Either you saw a ghost or you didn't."

Liza took a shaky breath before explaining. "Do you remember that skeleton in the band room?"

Melody nodded. "Mr. Belgrave called it Claude. Isn't it cute that he named him?"

Liza squeezed Melody's arm tight. "Only if you call a living skeleton cute!"

"A living skeleton?" Melody, Eddie, and Howie said together.

"You're nuts," Howie told her. "Claude is a science display. He's probably made out of plastic."

"Then what made Claude's toes tap along to our music?" Liza asked.

Eddie pecked Liza's forehead with his finger. "I think your brain has been tapped."

Liza knocked Eddie's hand away and frowned. "Remember, I was sitting next to that stack of bones. While you were blowing hot air into your instruments, something caught my attention. At first, I thought it was all your blowing moving a piece of paper on the floor. But then I looked closer. That's when I saw it."

"What?" Melody asked.

"Claude's toes were tapping out the same rhythm we were playing," Liza said. "And I saw it with my own eyes!"

"Maybe you need glasses," Howie suggested.

Melody nodded. "The only tapping going on was Mr. Belgrave's wand when he was trying to get Eddie's attention."

"But I saw it!" Liza insisted. "That skeleton was listening to us. It was like our music made him come to life."

"Are you saying our music was bad enough to wake the dead?" Eddie joked.

"Maybe," Liza said seriously. "Or maybe he was already alive."

Melody patted Liza on the back and ignored Eddie's giggles. "Claude can't be alive," she told Liza. "His toes were just wiggling from the vibrations of all the musical instruments."

Howie nodded. "Melody's right. A little vibration and a lot of imagination. That's all there is to it."

Just then, a low tune echoed down the hall. Liza rubbed the goose bumps on her arms and looked at her friends. "Then who's playing the tuba?" she asked softly.

6

Music Lessons

"I'm not sitting by Claude again," Liza hissed. It was the next day, and the third-graders at Bailey Elementary were waiting to file into the new band room.

Eddie rolled his eyes. "Don't worry, I don't think Claude is going to flirt with you."

"Tease all you want," Liza told him. "But there's something strange about that skeleton."

"Okay, okay," Eddie said. "I'll sit next to Claude just to keep you from complaining."

Mr. Belgrave handed each student their instrument as they walked in the door. Melody took her flute and waited for Liza to get her saxophone. Eddie grabbed his cymbals and Howie took his gleaming trombone. Claude stood in the back of the room, just like yesterday. Liza peered up at his blank grin and shivered. But Eddie just grinned back.

"Howdy, Claude," Eddie said. Then he reached out and shook the skeleton's bony hand.

A funny look came over Eddie's face, and he quickly let go of Claude's hand. "That's weird," he said. "His hand feels warm."

"So?" Melody asked.

Eddie shrugged. "I figured it'd be cold. After all, he isn't alive."

Howie sat in the chair next to Eddie and slid the slide on his trombone. "The sun shining through the window probably warmed it up."

Eddie nodded. "Right. That must be it." Then he giggled and sat down with his back to Claude. "I'm beginning to sound like Liza!"

Liza scowled at him, but she didn't

bother saying anything. Besides, Mr. Belgrave tapped his baton on his music stand, calling the class to order.

Mr. Belgrave stood up straight and raised the conductor's wand over his head, with his long skinny arms almost touching the ceiling. All the students lifted their instruments. As Mr. Belgrave dropped the wand in a graceful arch, the students began to play. Only the sound that came from the band room was nothing like music. It sounded more like fingernails scratching a chalkboard.

Mr. Belgrave shook his head and tapped his wand three times on the music stand. "Let's try that again," he suggested. "This time, stay together by watching my wand."

Again, Mr. Belgrave raised his wand high in the air and then let it fall. And again, the kids pounded, and blew, and tooted.

For nearly a half hour, the third-graders

worked on staying together and finding the right notes. But to Eddie, it sounded worse and worse. Of course, he wasn't having any trouble with his cymbals. He had already figured out the best way to bang the gleaming circles of brass together for the loudest crash.

While the rest of his friends were struggling with their instruments, Eddie looked around the old science room. Dusty beakers and test tubes lined the shelves and a broken film projector stood in the corner. A big silver tuba was squeezed in between Claude and the shelves. Eddie looked at Claude again. Something struck him as odd. Was it his imagination or had Claude's empty grin turned into a big frown?

Just then, Mr. Belgrave tapped his conducter's wand on the music stand and sighed. "No, no, no. You just don't seem to be getting it. Claude can play better than that. Let me show you."

The young musicians watched their new band teacher take long strides across the room and open a tall coat closet. He reached inside and pulled a shining trumpet from the shelf.

"You play the trumpet?" Carey, who was sitting in the front row, asked.

Mr. Belgrave smiled his yellow toothy smile and nodded. "Of course. This is my instrument of choice. I am especially moved by the sound of 'Taps' being played. Now, let me show you how to play 'The Bailey Elementary March.' "

Mr. Belgrave took a deep breath. His pale cheeks puffed as he blew and his fingers danced like spider legs on the valves of the trumpet. A smooth line of notes floated from the instrument, and even Eddie was impressed.

"Now watch again," Mr. Belgrave instructed them. "Notice how the notes

hang on to each other like they belong together."

With another deep breath, he played the melody as the children listened. It was a catchy tune, with notes that went high and then low like a roller coaster. Melody moved her head to the beat and Liza was swaying with the music.

"Quit tapping me," Eddie hissed to Howie. Eddie felt the drumming of his friend's fingers on his back. "You're giving me a headache."

But Howie was too busy watching Mr. Belgrave to pay any attention to Eddie. The annoying tapping continued.

Eddie elbowed his friend. "I said to stop!"

This time Howie looked at Eddie. "I'm not doing anything to you!" Then Howie went back to watching Mr. Belgrave.

Eddie sat very still. If it wasn't Howie

tapping him on the shoulder, who was it? Eddie stiffly turned his head and looked over his shoulder, right into the grinning face of Claude.

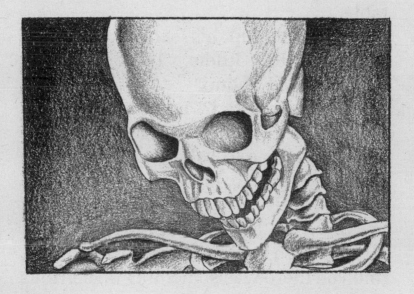

7

Dancing Skeletons

"I'm telling you Liza is right!" Eddie screeched at his friends across the lunch table.

Howie held up his sandwich. "Calm down," he told Eddie. "There's nothing to get excited about."

"Don't get excited?" Eddie squealed. "A skeleton was trying to dance with me and you tell me to calm down!"

"There's got to be a logical explanation," Melody said, wiping the milk off her face with a paper napkin.

Liza folded her arms across her chest. "I told you there was something mysterious about that skeleton, but you wouldn't listen."

Eddie rolled his eyes. "It kills me to say

this, but you were right. That skeleton is alive!"

Howie dropped his sandwich onto his lunch tray. "Hold on just a minute. Mr. Belgrave may be a little strange, and he definitely needs to find a good dentist to clean those yellow teeth. . . ."

"But he doesn't have living skeletons in his band room," Melody interrupted.

Eddie pointed his straw at Melody. "How can you be so sure? After all, remember where we first saw him?"

"In the cemetery," Liza whispered, her face pale.

"Exactly." Eddie nodded. "And it doesn't take a rocket scientist to know that there are skeletons in cemeteries. I'm telling you we've got to do something about Mr. Belgrave and Claude."

Howie gulped down another bite of his sandwich. "I think you're getting all excited over nothing."

"You won't think it's nothing when all

the skeletons in the Bailey City Cemetery come to life! Mr. Belgrave may even be planning on turning us into skeletons!" Eddie said seriously. "We need to stay away from him."

Howie and Melody both laughed but they stopped short when they heard a strange moaning sound.

"It's the tuba again," Liza said softly.

"It must be Mr. Belgrave," Melody said. "I bet he was lying about not being able to play the tuba."

Eddie shook his head and pointed across the room. "It's not Mr. Belgrave. He's over there." The four friends stared at their tall, skinny band teacher getting lettuce from the salad bar.

"I bet Claude is playing it," Liza said softly. "Remember Mr. Belgrave said Claude could play the song better than us."

Eddie, Melody, and Howie looked at Liza in surprise.

Melody rolled her eyes. "You're crazy," she said.

"It can't be Claude." Howie shook his head. "Skeletons don't play tubas."

"It is Claude," Eddie agreed firmly. "And I'm going to prove it!"

8

Special Guest

As soon as they got back to their classroom, Liza whispered to Eddie. "How are you going to prove that Claude is alive?"

Eddie shook his head. "I don't know yet, but I'll figure out something. You try to. . ."

"Shhh," Liza said. "Mrs. Jeepers is looking at us."

Their teacher, Mrs. Jeepers, smiled her odd little half smile at Eddie as if she knew all of their secrets. "I have a wonderful surprise," she told the class in her thick Transylvanian accent. "Our new band teacher has chosen our class to perform at the upcoming Fall Festival. He's asked for extra practice time and I have agreed."

A few kids in the class clapped, but Eddie and Liza slumped down in their seats. "So much for staying away from him," Liza muttered.

Mrs. Jeepers flashed her green eyes and continued. "Mr. Belgrave has also informed me that a very special surprise guest will be performing with you at the festival."

"Who is it?" Melody asked with her hand raised.

"I cannot tell you that," Mrs. Jeepers said, rubbing her brooch. "If I told you, it would ruin the surprise."

"That's okay," Eddie said. "I don't like surprises anyway."

Mrs. Jeepers looked at Eddie and rubbed her brooch. "I will give you one clue," she said.

"What?" Howie asked.

"The surprise performer will play the tuba," Mrs. Jeepers said in her strange accent.

Eddie heard a loud noise and looked around. Liza had fallen out of her chair

and was sitting on the floor with books scattered all around her.

Mrs. Jeepers rushed over. "Are you all right?" she asked, helping Liza back into her seat.

"I . . . I . . . I think so," Liza stuttered. "I just felt funny there for a moment."

"I know what's wrong," Eddie told Mrs. Jeepers. "Liza hit her funny bones the wrong way."

Liza looked at Eddie. "It's bones, all right," she said, "but there is nothing funny about it."

That afternoon at recess, the four friends gathered under the big oak tree on the playground. Liza was about to cry. "Mr. Belgrave is going to have Claude play at the Fall Festival!"

"Don't be ridiculous," Melody told her.

"Who else can play the tuba?" Liza asked. "I don't want to play in the festival if I have to play with a skeleton."

"Don't worry about it," Eddie said. "I've figured out a way to get to the bottom of this bony business."

"What are you going to do?" Howie asked.

"I'll explain everything," Eddie told them. Even though the rest of the third-graders were screaming on the jungle gym, Eddie was careful to whisper his plan. Howie, Melody, and Liza leaned close so they could hear.

Liza shivered. "I hope you know what you're doing. If I hear Claude playing the tuba one more time, I think I'll turn into a skeleton myself."

9

Night School

That evening, dark storm clouds hung low over Bailey City and lightning streaked across the sky. A cold autumn wind rattled the branches of the oak tree, sending withered leaves floating to the ground near the four huddled friends. Liza pulled her coat tight about her before she faced Eddie. "Are you sure this is a good idea?" she asked.

Melody nodded. "We could get into trouble."

"*Big* trouble," Howie added.

Eddie glanced at the dark windows of Bailey Elementary. "We'll be in bigger trouble if we don't. Besides, this is the perfect time."

"How do you figure that?" Melody asked.

"Listen," Eddie said.

Howie, Melody, and Liza stood as still as statues. They heard muffled music floating from the empty building. "Someone is playing the tuba," Eddie said, "and I think it's Claude."

Without another word, Eddie stalked across the playground and pulled open the side door to the school. "How did you know it'd be open?" Howie asked.

"I knew the janitor would still be here," Eddie whispered as he went in the door. Once inside, the four friends stopped long enough to let their eyes get used to the dark hall. Thunder made the windows rattle and drifting clouds cast long shadows on the black-and-white floor.

"We should have brought a flashlight," Liza whimpered.

"I have a flashlight," Howie said, reaching into his pocket.

"No," Eddie said softly. "We have to

surprise him. A flashlight would be like an invitation to a funeral. Our funeral. Now, let's go."

Carefully, Eddie led his friends down the hall. Melody walked beside Eddie with Howie close behind. Liza took her time. She didn't like the darkness or the music echoing through the deserted school. The tuba notes sounded like the beating heart of a monster and they grew louder and louder as the four friends got closer to the old science lab. They were almost there when . . .

Wham! Liza found herself sprawled on the floor. She screamed just to make sure she was still alive. She had been so busy peering over her shoulder that she hadn't seen the swinging door sticking out into the hall. Instead of walking around it like her friends, she had crashed right into the door, slamming it shut.

Everyone froze.

"Shhhh!" Eddie warned. But it was too late. The music stopped, filling the halls of Bailey Elementary with a deadly silence.

Melody grabbed Liza's arm and pulled her into a nearby janitor's closet. "She didn't mean to do it," Melody whispered to Eddie as the kids hid.

"She should have watched where she was going," Eddie snapped.

Liza sniffed and wiped a tear from her cheek while Howie peeked out the closet door toward the band room. "Maybe he didn't hear us," Howie suggested. "The door is still closed, nobody left."

"Of course nobody heard," Eddie muttered. "Claude has 'no body.'"

Melody patted Liza on the shoulder. "We should forget this boneheaded plan and get home," Melody told Eddie, "before Liza's nose starts bleeding."

Liza nodded. Her nose often bled when she was upset, and she was plenty nervous right now. "I hear Claude coming to get us!" she whimpered.

Howie slapped his forehead. "That was just me cracking my knuckles. Next, you'll think Melody's chattering teeth is Claude doing a tap dance!"

"You still don't believe Claude is alive, do you?" Eddie asked his friend.

"Of course not," Howie said. "I don't believe in ghouls or zombies or living, breathing skeletons."

"Then you won't mind walking down that hall and taking a look in the band room?" Eddie asked.

Howie peeked out of the closet again and down the long, dark hallway. It looked like a big black mouth waiting to swallow him up, but he wasn't about to let his friends see him scared.

"I'll go," Howie told him. "But you have

to come with me. And bring the flashlight."

Eddie barely nodded. "Let's do it." They slipped out of the closet with Melody and Liza right behind them.

There was no music now. The only sound was the thunder rumbling over the Red River. Howie drew a deep breath before pulling open the band room door. There, glowing in the dim flashlight, was Claude and he was holding the tuba.

"Run!" Howie screamed. At least, he tried to scream but it sounded more like a bullfrog croaking under water. But his friends knew what he meant, and they tore down the hall like they were racing lightning.

"This way!" Liza screamed. She led her friends around a corner and toward an exit sign. Heavy footsteps echoed behind them.

"Hurry!" Melody gasped. "Before that skeleton makes mincemeat out of us."

Liza crashed against the door, frantically pushing the handle. "It's locked," she cried.

The four friends backed against the locked door and faced the long, dark corridor. "We have to find another way out!" Howie sputtered.

"It's too late," Eddie said as the heavy footsteps came closer.

10

Skull

"Oh my gosh," Liza squealed before ducking behind Melody. "I see his skull!"

In a flash of lightning, the kids did see a skull. But they also saw round glasses and an egg-shaped body.

"Principal Davis!" Howie said in relief. "What are you doing here?"

Principal Davis scratched his bald head. "I was going to ask you the same question. After all, school was over hours ago."

Eddie was used to fibbing to the principal. "Oh, we came by to get our spelling books so we could study."

Principal Davis nodded his head slowly. "I'm glad that you wanted to study, but it's too late now. Go home and go to bed. Get plenty of rest. Don't forget the Fall Festival is tomorrow."

"Yes, sir," Melody said, eager to get out of the school.

Principal Davis pulled a ring of keys from his pocket to unlock the door. "Don't let me catch you in here again so late," he warned.

"No, sir," Eddie said innocently as the four kids trotted out the door.

But Liza couldn't leave without asking Principal Davis a question. "Did you hear music?" she asked.

"Music?" Principal Davis said, smiling. "Perhaps you heard my radio. I just love listening to band music. The sound of a brass instrument just sends chills up my spine."

"Mine too," Eddie muttered when Principal Davis closed the door.

Thunder rumbled as the kids gathered under the oak tree. "Let's get home," Liza said. "It's going to storm any minute."

"But first, we have to figure out how to

save the school from Claude," Eddie told his friends.

Melody pulled her jacket tighter. "You heard Principal Davis. It was just his radio we heard."

Eddie shook his head. "I don't think so."

"A radio makes perfect sense," Melody insisted.

"I'm beginning to wonder," Howie said. "Even Mrs. Jeepers said it was tuba music. And don't forget we saw Claude holding the tuba with our own eyes."

"And he was glowing!" Liza shuddered. "I know it was him chasing us. There's no telling what would have happened if Principal Davis hadn't come along."

Howie nodded. "This is getting stranger and stranger. I think we need to get to the bottom of this whole thing."

"Before Bailey City has skeletons walking the streets," Eddie agreed. The four kids started walking slowly home, trying to think of a plan. But when a loud moaning sound came from the school, they jumped.

"The tuba!" Liza screeched. The four friends ran down the street.

11

Believe It or Not

"Pssst!" Howie peeked around from behind the oak tree the next morning before school, motioning for Eddie and Liza to join him. "I've figured out a solution to our skeleton scare," he told his friends. "We don't have a thing to worry about."

Howie reached into a brown paper bag and pulled out a long knotted string. "This is for you," he told Liza. "And here's one for Eddie."

Eddie slapped his forehead. "Great! I'm supposed to protect myself from a killer skeleton with a piece of twine! What am I going to do? Floss his knuckles?"

Howie didn't laugh. "Don't worry, Bone Brains, there's more. Much more." But before he could pull anything else from his bag of tricks, Melody looked around the huge tree trunk.

"What are you guys up to?" she asked. "You're going to be late for class if you don't hurry."

Liza grabbed Melody's coat sleeve and pulled her around the oak tree. "Howie has a plan to protect us from Claude."

Melody giggled. "A marshmallow could protect us from that stack of bones."

"If you don't believe in living skeletons, then you won't mind wearing this," Howie told her. He pulled a tiny paper jack-o'-lantern out of his crinkled bag.

Melody sat down on the brown grass and giggled. "Why would I want to wear an itty-bitty pumpkin?"

"Remember what Mrs. Jeepers said? Jack-o'-lanterns are supposed to ward off evil spirits," Howie said matter-of-factly.

"They haven't gotten rid of Eddie yet," Melody kidded. "And Claude is nothing to be afraid of compared to Eddie!"

Howie stared hard at Melody. "This is no joking matter. Jack-o'-lanterns were originally used to get rid of dead spirits, and I can't think of anything deader than a skeleton."

"But Claude is just the remains of an old science kit," Melody argued.

"Old science kits don't do bone dances on kids' backs," Eddie disagreed. "I think we'd better listen to Howie."

Howie handed the paper jack-o'-lantern and string to Melody. "After all, it won't hurt to wear this around your neck," he said, "even if you don't believe. And if what Mrs. Jeepers said is true, it'll put a muffler on Claude. It'll prove that he's alive!"

"The only thing this proves is that you have a cracked skull yourself," Melody told Howie. But she threaded the twine through a hole in the pumpkin stem and put the homemade necklace over her neck. Liza and Eddie did the same.

Liza's eyes grew big. "But what if Mrs. Jeepers sees them? I don't think she wants jack-o'-lanterns in the classroom."

Howie nodded. "I remembered. I made them small so we can hide them under our shirts. Now, let's go."

Once inside the classroom, the four friends slid into their seats and started their day's work. Mrs. Jeepers was known for giving more assignments than any other teacher at Bailey Elementary. It was hard to work, knowing that the Fall Festival was just a few hours away, but the third-graders opened their books and got busy anyway. Nobody dared upset Mrs. Jeepers.

They were halfway done with their math when Howie kicked Melody in the shin. "Did you notice something?" he whispered.

Melody glanced at Mrs. Jeepers to make

sure she wasn't looking, but the third-grade teacher was busy helping Carey multiply three numbers together. Melody shook her head to answer Howie.

"It's quiet," he told her.

"So?" Melody shrugged. "Mrs. Jeepers's room is always quiet."

"The rest of the school is silent, too," Howie pointed out. "There's no tuba music!"

Melody's mouth dropped open, but Howie didn't notice. "I was right," he hissed. "The jack-o'-lanterns are working." He smiled and pulled out his tiny necklace to prove his point.

But Howie's face turned a shade of green when long white fingers reached from behind him and slowly circled his wrist.

Mrs. Jeepers stood in front of Howie. "I do not want these in my classroom," she said in her thick accent. "There are many other decorations of the fall season. Please take those necklaces off." Mrs. Jeepers touched her green brooch and flashed her eyes at the other children. Slowly Melody, Liza, Howie, and Eddie gave their necklaces to their teacher.

12

Doomed

"Now what are we going to do?" Liza moaned at the lunch table. "The Fall Festival is less than an hour away and we don't have our jack-o'-lanterns. Mrs. Jeepers locked them in her drawer."

"Maybe we could make some more?" Howie suggested.

"There's no time," Liza whimpered.

Eddie shot his straw wrapper at Howie. "If Bone Head here hadn't been showing off, we'd have been okay."

"We have nothing to worry about," Melody defended Howie. "After all, it's been quiet all day."

Eddie looked hopeful. "Maybe old 'Claude without a bod' knows we're on to him and decided to keep his mouth shut."

The kids nodded and bit into their pizza slices without another thought to skeleton bones, alive or dead. But as they lined up to go to the festival, Claude was on their minds again. Long, sad tuba notes echoed down the halls of Bailey Elementary.

"Oh, no!" Liza cried. "It's Claude. Just in time for the festival!"

The kids had no choice but to file into the gymnasium behind Mrs. Jeepers. There, sitting on the stage, for everyone to see, was Claude. He was holding the tuba and he was smiling!

Mrs. Jeepers turned to her students and smiled. "Good luck, ladies and gentlemen. You are the first to perform. You may go on the stage now."

Liza shook her head and hid behind Melody. "There's no way I'm going on that stage."

Mrs. Jeepers smiled her strange little half smile. "No need to be afraid. Every-

one has had stage fright from time to time. Let me help you." She grabbed Liza's hand and pulled her up onto the stage with the rest of the class following. Mrs. Jeepers sat Liza right in front of Claude and patted her on the shoulder.

"I think my nose is going to bleed," Liza whined.

"Do not worry," Mrs. Jeepers said as she stepped to the side of the stage. "You will do fine."

Mr. Belgrave stood in front of the class and tapped his conductor's baton on a music stand. The students picked up their instruments and began playing "The Bailey Elementary March." The students played their best and Mr. Belgrave smiled a big yellow-toothed smile.

Halfway through the song, low sad notes came from behind Liza's chair. Liza gulped and almost dropped her saxophone. When the song was over, everyone in the audience clapped and cheered.

Mrs. Jeepers smiled her odd little half smile and nodded. Liza smiled back and bowed with the rest of the class. Then very slowly, she turned to look behind her. What she saw almost made her faint.

13

Two Bald Heads

Instead of one bald head behind Liza, there were two. One belonged to Claude and the other one belonged to Principal Davis. Both of them were smiling, but now Principal Davis had the tuba wrapped around him.

"How did you like my surprise?" Principal Davis asked Liza. "I bet you didn't know your old principal could toot a horn."

Liza shook her head with relief but Eddie stepped up beside her. "I knew it was you playing the tuba all along," Eddie bragged.

"You did not!" Melody put her hands on her hips and looked at Eddie. "You thought Claude was playing."

Eddie's face turned bright red to match

his hair. "I did not!" he lied. "After all, skeletons don't play tubas."

Mrs. Jeepers came up beside Eddie. "I did not know you were so interested in skeletons," she told him. "You will be delighted with our new science unit."

Eddie shook his head. "Science has never delighted me before."

Mrs. Jeepers touched her green brooch and smiled. "You will like this," she said with certainty.

"What will we be studying?" Melody asked.

"The human skeleton," Mrs. Jeepers said.

Eddie didn't say anything as everyone around him laughed. But he gulped when he thought he saw Claude wink at him.